BEFORE I MADE HISTORY

Lead Us to Freedom, Harriet Tubman!

by Peter and Connie Roop

SCHOLASTIC INC.

New York   Toronto   London   Auckland   Sydney
Mexico City   New Delhi   Hong Kong   Buenos Aires

ISBN 0-439-79255-X

12 11 10 9   14 15 16/0

Printed in the U.S.A.   40
First printing, January 2006

For our Harriet, Ron and All That Jazz!

Contents

Introduction

When Harriet Tubman was born, her parents named her Harriet after her mother. Did you know that her family usually called her Minty?

Harriet was born a slave. Did you know that she ran away to be free?

Harriet Tubman never went to school. Did you know she never learned to read or write?

Harriet ran away when she was an adult. Did you know that the first time she tried to run away she was only seven years old?

When Harriet Tubman was about fifteen years old, she almost died. Did you know that she survived and lived to be more than ninety years old?

Harriet married John Tubman. Did you know that he was not a slave like Harriet was?

Harriet Tubman led more than three hundred slaves to freedom on the Underground Railroad. Did you know she never lost a single one of her passengers along the way?

Harriet Tubman could not read a map. Did you know that she used the North Star to help her from getting lost?

Harriet Tubman wore disguises. Did you know she often dressed like a man?

Harriet Tubman is famous for helping hundreds of slaves escape to freedom. Did you know that during the Civil War she was also a spy and a nurse?

The answers to these questions and many more lie in who Harriet Tubman was as a girl and young woman. This book is about Harriet Tubman before she made history.

1

Harriet Tubman Is Born

Candles burned brightly in the windows of the "Big House." Master Edward Brodess and his family lived in the Big House. The Brodess plantation was near Bucktown, Maryland, on the eastern shore of Chesapeake Bay. Bucktown was a small town with a store, a post office, and a few homes.

No candles burned in Rit and Ben's one-room cabin. Their cabin was down in the slave quarters behind the Big House. Master Brodess owned Rit. Her husband, Ben, was owned by another master.

Candles were too expensive to burn in a slave's cabin. Candles were only for the Big House. But a fire flickered in Ben and Rit's small fireplace.

Rit lay on a pile of blankets. There was no bed in the cabin. Rit gently rocked her new baby girl. She was the eleventh child Rit and Ben had brought into the world.

Ben sat on the floor. There were no chairs. He smiled as he looked at his wife and their new baby.

Rit and Ben named their daughter Harriet. Harriet was Rit's real name. Over time, her owners had shortened Harriet to Rit. Baby Harriet was given her father's last name of Ross. Harriet Ross. One day, she would be known as Harriet Tubman.

Other slaves heard that Ben and Rit had another child. Quietly, they came in the dark to see the newborn baby. They had waited until their work in the fields, in the kitchen, in the barn, or in the Big House was finished.

Slaves often gave their children "cradle names" or nicknames. Harriet's parents called her Araminta. But before long, her family was calling her Minty for short.

Minty had ten brothers and sisters. Some of them lived in the slave quarters.

Master Brodess sent some of these family members to work on other plantations. These planters paid him money to rent his slaves to work for them. When the job was finished, the slaves returned to the Brodess plantation. They were still Master Brodess's slaves.

Minty never knew some of her other sisters and brothers. They had been sold to masters far away down south. Being "sold south" meant a slave never saw any of his or her family again. Minty's parents hoped she would never be sold south. Although life as a slave in Maryland was hard, working on a cotton or rice plantation down south was much worse.

Even though Rit and Ben were owned by different masters, they shared a cabin. Their masters respected their hard work and let them have this small benefit. Ben and Rit did their best to give their children a loving home. But no matter what, Master Brodess owned his slaves. He could sell Ben and Rit's children any time he wanted to.

No one knows for sure when Minty was

born. The slaves themselves could not read or write. Minty's birth meant Master Brodess owned another slave. He could keep her, sell her, or hire her out. If Minty lived to be old enough to work, Master Brodess would then write her name in his record book. This is where he listed his slaves along with the cows, horses, pigs, and other things he owned.

Most likely, Minty was born in 1820 or 1821. Even though her birthday was never recorded, the day Harriet Tubman died in 1913 was known across America. Harriet Tubman was remembered as a brave, strong, courageous woman who led hundreds of slaves like herself to freedom.

2
Minty Grows Up

The Brodess plantation was Minty's only world for her first five years. Life was not easy for any slaves, but here she learned to walk and talk and laugh and sing. Here she ran and played with the other slave children.

She learned how her grandparents had been captured in Africa. She heard the terrible stories of the long time they spent chained on a ship coming to America. She heard how they were forced into slavery.

She listened to stories of slaves who had escaped to freedom. They had gone north to states like Pennsylvania where slavery was not allowed. Minty learned what happened to slaves who were caught. They were returned to their masters and were whipped or beaten.

Minty heard the sad stories of her brothers and sisters who had been sold to owners far away.

Minty was proud of one story about her mother. Rit was determined to try to keep her remaining family together, even if she got into trouble. One day, Rit found out that one of her sons was going to be sold. Master Brodess needed some extra money. The boy would be taken south to Georgia and sold to a new owner.

Rit didn't want to lose another child, so she came up with a plan. Rit hid her son in the woods.

When Master Brodess went to Rit and Ben's cabin, the boy wasn't there. He demanded the boy be turned over. Brave Rit picked up an ax and said, "No!"

Master Brodess gave up. He didn't want to hurt Rit. She had worked hard for him. He realized that selling this boy was not worth all the trouble. He could do without the money. When Rit realized her son was safe, she brought him home. Master Brodess even

told Rit he was glad she hid the boy because he didn't really want to sell him in the first place.

These stories, songs, and maybe a cornhusk doll were the few things Minty could call her own. Everything else belonged to Master Brodess.

The slaves did not have nice clothes to wear. Young Minty wore a dress that had been made out of an old sack. Minty didn't even have shoes to wear. In winter and in summer, she went barefoot like all the other slave children.

Minty ate what the other slaves ate. At one meal, she might have only corn bread. Sometimes she might have a tiny bit of pork. There were usually beans, potatoes, or other vegetables grown on the plantation. Or there might be a fish someone in her family caught.

When she was small, Minty slept in a cradle her father had made. When she was bigger, Minty slept on a pile of blankets like the rest of her family did.

Minty's father, Ben, was a skilled woodsman. He knew which of the tall oaks, cypresses, and poplars would make the best boards. He swung his heavy ax day after day, cutting down trees for his master. The valuable logs were shipped across Chesapeake Bay. Then the logs were cut into boards for ships, homes, and furniture.

Ben was so good at his job that his master put him in charge of the other slaves cutting down trees. Ben was fair to the men who helped him. He was known to be very honest. It was said that no one ever heard Ben Ross tell a lie.

Minty's mother worked in the Big House. She might have cooked for her master and his family. She might have swept the floors, dusted the furniture, made the beds, done the dishes and the laundry. Minty didn't see the jobs her mother did. She just watched Rit go to the Big House early every morning. And she waited for her parents to return at sundown.

3
Minty Works Away
from Home

While her parents worked, Minty was left in the care of a slave woman too old to work anymore. Minty played with the other young slaves. She listened to the tales the old woman told. When it was cold, they stayed in one of the slave cabins. When it was warm, they played outside.

When Minty was about six years old, her life changed. Now she was old enough to work, so Master Brodess sent her to work on another farm.

This farm was owned by James Cook. Mrs. Cook wanted a child slave like Minty to help her weave cotton into cloth. She knew she wouldn't have to pay Master Brodess too

13

much for a young slave girl. Master Brodess would keep the money. All Minty would get were old clothes and a little food.

Minty had no choice. She had to go work for the Cooks. As soon as she got into the wagon that was taking her away from the Brodess plantation, Minty began to miss her family.

Life was hard for Minty at the Cooks'. She slept on the kitchen floor. Sometimes she moved near the fireplace. She put her bare feet into the ashes to keep them warm. Mrs. Cook fed her scraps left from the family meals. Minty ate her food alone outside.

Mrs. Cook tried to teach Minty how to wind yarn. After Mrs. Cook spun cotton into yarn, Minty would try to wind the yarn. But it was hard work for her small hands. Minty often made mistakes. She had to wind the yarn over and over again. This made Mrs. Cook very angry.

Finally, Mrs. Cook told her husband that Minty was useless. Mr. Cook decided Minty might be able to help him.

The Cook plantation was near a river where muskrats swam. Mr. Cook set traps to catch them in the fall when their fur was thick. He sold the fur to make hats and coats.

Trapping muskrats was hard work. Someone had to wade into the cold water to pull up the traps. The muskrats had to be taken out of the traps and put into a sack. Then the traps had to be put back into the water.

Mr. Cook gave this difficult job to Minty. For long hours, she waded in the chilly water taking care of the traps.

As hard as the work was, Minty liked being outside. She enjoyed the sun, wind, and the fresh air. She was away from Mrs. Cook's angry voice. She was also away from the cotton lint floating in the cabin. The lint made Minty sneeze.

But when winter came, trapping muskrats was even more difficult. The water was icy cold. Since Minty had no shoes, her bare feet were wet and cold all day. She had no coat to keep her warm. Before long, Minty began to cough and sneeze. She developed a high

fever. She broke out in red spots. Minty had the measles.

Mrs. Cook refused to take care of a sick slave child. She sent Minty back to the Brodess plantation, complaining that she was worthless. Rit lovingly cared for her sick daughter. Slowly, she nursed Minty back to health.

When Minty was well, Master Brodess sent her to work on another plantation. This time, Minty worked for someone she called Miss Susan.

Miss Susan had just had a baby. She needed Minty to take care of her baby. She also wanted her to help with the housework.

Minty helped cook and clean. She served meals. She took care of the baby when Miss Susan was busy. Minty was so small, she had to sit on the floor to safely hold the baby.

4
Minty Runs Away

After working all day, Minty had to take care of the baby at night. When the baby needed changing, Minty had to get up and change the diapers. When the baby cried, Minty quickly tried to rock it back to sleep. If the baby woke up Miss Susan, Minty would be whipped.

One day, Miss Susan was especially mean. She whipped Minty five times before breakfast! Minty had scars from those beatings all her life.

Minty learned a trick. When she thought she was going to be whipped, she put on every bit of clothing she could find. Then the whipping didn't hurt as much. Later, Minty took off the extra clothes so she could do her jobs.

The hard work and lack of sleep made Minty sick again. Miss Susan sent her back home. Even as sick as she was, Minty was glad to be with her family again.

Once more, Rit nursed Minty back to health. And again, when Minty was well enough to work, she was rented to another owner.

One day, the mistress Minty worked for had an argument with her husband. Minty stood by the kitchen table. She looked down at the sugar bowl. Even though she was seven years old, Minty had never tasted sugar before. When the wife wasn't looking, Minty put her fingers into the sugar bowl. She wanted just one little taste.

But the angry wife saw her and grabbed her whip! Minty hated being whipped. Without thinking, she ran out the kitchen door. She ran across the yard. She ran and ran until she was worn out. She saw a pigpen. Inside the pen, a mother pig and her babies were eating scraps of food. Minty was so hungry and tired, she climbed into the pigpen.

Minty hid in the pigpen for four days. She was cold and hungry, but she stayed. She had to fight the pigs for even a tiny bit of food. She was homesick for her family.

Finally, Minty gave up. She returned to the farmhouse. She was too tired and hungry to care if she was whipped or not.

Once more, Minty was sent back to Master Brodess. By now, he realized that Minty was not good at working inside homes. So he sent her out to work in the fields.

Field work was hard work. Minty worked from sunrise to sunset. She cut wheat. She planted corn. She harvested fruits and vegetables. She drove oxen. She plowed fields. She lifted heavy barrels into wagons.

By the time she was eleven years old, Minty was strong and healthy. Now Master Brodess rented her out only to help with field work. Minty didn't mind this hard work. She would rather work outside than inside.

Minty was learning other things besides hard work. It was against the law for slaves to learn to read and write, so Minty never went to school. At home, Rit told Minty stories from the Bible. Minty's religious beliefs grew strong, too.

Ben, however, became Minty's best teacher. On Sundays, when the slaves had their one day off, Ben and Minty wandered in the woods. Ben showed Minty how to walk quietly without snapping a stick. He showed her where to find fresh, clean water to drink. He told her which plants she could eat and which plants would hurt her. He showed her how to make medicines out of some plants.

Ben taught her how to fish with a string and bent nail. He showed her how the tides from Chesapeake Bay moved north up the river.

5
Minty Is Hurt

Minty liked learning Ben's lessons about the woods. She also liked looking at the stars on clear nights with her father. One night, Ben taught Minty a special lesson about the stars.

Ben pointed out seven stars in the sky. He told her they were shaped liked a drinking gourd. The slaves used a gourd to drink water from a bucket.

Minty saw the drinking-gourd shape. Ben told her to imagine water pouring out of the drinking gourd. She did. Ben said that there was a bright star where the pouring water went. She saw it. Ben told Minty that this bright star was the North Star. The other

stars might move, he said, but the North Star always pointed north.

Minty knew that north meant freedom. She heard other slaves talk about "following the drinking gourd" to freedom. But Minty knew a slave had to run away to follow the drinking gourd.

Minty also heard tales of a strange railroad to freedom. It was called the Underground Railroad. Minty learned that it was not a real railroad with trains and tracks. Instead, it was a special way that slaves could escape to freedom in the North.

Minty heard that people—called "conductors"—led escaping slaves from one safe place to another. Each safe place was a stop or a "station" along the Underground Railroad. The people at the stations were called "stationmasters." Minty learned that many of the conductors and stationmasters were white people. Minty was surprised to find out that some white people believed that slavery was wrong. She was excited to learn that these people risked their lives to help slaves run away to freedom in the North.

Minty thought about the muskrats. She remembered how they were trapped just like she was. She thought about the geese that were free to fly north in the spring. *Maybe one day, I'll set myself free and fly north, too,* she thought.

But Minty had little time to dream of freedom. After a hard day in the fields, Minty usually fell asleep right after dinner.

When Minty was about thirteen years old, she was working on Mr. Barrett's farm. She noticed a fellow slave acting strangely. Suddenly, the slave began running away.

Minty saw the white man in charge of the slaves leave to go after the runaway. Minty guessed the slave might be trying to get to Bucktown. Minty raced ahead to warn the slave the man was after him.

The runaway slave dashed into a store. The white man ran in after him. Minty ran into the store, too. When the slave ran out the door, Minty stood in the doorway to block the white man's path.

The man was angry. He picked up a heavy piece of metal. He threw it at the escaping slave. He missed the slave, but the metal hit Minty in the head. She was knocked out and fell to the floor. Minty was carried home, and she didn't wake up for two days!

Rit cared for her injured daughter. Slowly, Minty's health returned. But something was wrong with Minty's head. Her injury made Minty fall asleep at odd times. She might be talking with someone and fall asleep for twenty minutes. Then she would wake up and keep talking. After several long months, Minty was finally well enough to work. But the sleeping spells would continue all her life.

Minty was also left with a scar on the side of her head. She began wrapping a piece of cloth around her head to make a turban. The turban hid the scar.

Master Brodess tried to sell Minty, but nobody wanted to buy an injured slave. One day, John Stewart came to see Master Brodess. Minty's father worked for Mr. Stewart in his lumber business. He asked if Minty could join her father in the forest. Master Brodess agreed. Minty was soon swinging an ax beside her father, cutting down Mr. Stewart's tall trees.

6
Minty Plans to Follow the Drinking Gourd

Minty was pleased to be working outside. She chopped long logs into smaller logs. She drove oxen to pull the logs out of the forest. She cut firewood. Her strength and health returned.

Minty worked so hard that Mr. Stewart paid her for the extra work she did. After a year, Minty had enough money to buy some cattle of her own.

Minty had the reputation of being stronger than some men. Sometimes, when Mr. Stewart had guests, he made Minty pull a boat filled with rocks. Minty was hitched to the boat like an ox. Mr. Stewart then ordered her to pull. Minty hated doing this. But she had no choice because she was a slave. At times like this, Minty became even more determined to "follow the drinking gourd."

Minty's life remained much the same for the next ten years. She worked outside for different plantation owners. She helped her parents as they grew older.

But then her life changed. She met John Tubman. He was African-American, like Harriet, but he was not a slave. He was free. They probably met when Minty was cutting trees for Mr. Stewart.

Minty was amazed that John knew how to read and write. He told her stories and read books to her. John was impressed by Minty's strength. He liked her independent spirit, too.

After getting to know each other better, Minty and John decided to get married. They called it "jumping the broom" because they jumped over a broom as part of the ceremony. It was an African tradition.

Minty and John were married in 1844. There was no official record of their marriage.

Few written records of special times existed in the lives of African-Americans, whether they were free like John, or slaves like Minty.

Because Minty was a slave, John had to live with her on her owner's plantation.

One day, Minty told John about her dream of freedom. She explained that she wanted to run away. She planned to "follow the drinking gourd" north.

John did not like Minty's plan. He said he would not help her escape. He even said that he would tell her master what she was planning to do.

Minty was upset. She had expected John to help her. After all, he was free. He knew how freedom felt. She was especially angry that he would tell her owner about her plans. Other owners would be warned to look for her. Minty knew the slave catchers would quickly be on her trail when she ran away.

But Minty would not give up her dream. She decided that if John wouldn't help her run away, he could just stay behind.

In 1849, Minty realized that she could not

wait any longer. Master Brodess died and she learned that his family needed money. She was going to be sold!

Minty said, "There was one of two things I had a right to, liberty or death. If I could not have one, I would have the other."

Minty chose to grab the chance to be free. She knew she had to run away soon. But she didn't want to go alone. Since her husband was not willing to help her run away, Minty asked three of her brothers to join her. They agreed.

Late one night, while John Tubman was sound asleep, Minty slipped out of their cabin. She looked up and saw the "drinking gourd." She knew which way to go.

Minty met her brothers in the woods. Almost immediately, she knew it was a mistake to bring them. Minty remembered how her father taught her to walk quietly, but her brothers crashed through the woods. Minty pointed out the "drinking gourd," but her siblings worried that they were lost. They complained that they would be in big trouble if they were caught. She tried to reassure them that they wouldn't get caught if they just kept going.

Minty finally gave up. They hadn't gone very far at all. Her brothers were no help. But she knew she wasn't ready to go on alone. Sadly, Minty went back to her cabin. John Tubman never knew she had even left.

7
Minty Becomes
Harriet Tubman

One evening, Minty heard some terrible news. She and two of her brothers were going to be sold the very next day!

Again, Minty decided she would be free or die trying. And this time, she would escape alone.

But Minty wanted to let someone in her family know her plans. She couldn't tell her brothers. She couldn't tell her parents. She knew her father would never lie, not even to protect her. If he was asked where Minty was, he would have to tell the truth.

Minty had an idea. She walked past her sister Mary Ann's cabin. She began singing a song about going to the "Promised Land," a place of happiness in the Bible. Minty knew that Mary Ann would know her voice. She knew Mary Ann would understand that the "Promised Land" meant freedom up north. When Minty sang "Bound for Promised Land," Mary Ann knew she was running away to freedom.

This time, Minty was better prepared. She packed food and she took a quilt she had made. It was one of her few belongings. When John was asleep, she slipped away into the night.

Instead of running into the woods, Minty had a better plan this time. She went to the home of a white woman. Minty knew that this woman helped runaway slaves.

The kind woman invited Minty into her kitchen. She told Minty the names of two families who would help her escape. She told Minty how to reach the first house. Without realizing it, Minty had begun her first of many trips on the Underground Railroad.

Minty was to travel north, following the

Choptank River. She would cross into the state of Delaware. Delaware still allowed slavery, so she had to be careful. Near Camden, Delaware, Minty was to look for a white farmhouse with green shutters.

Minty wanted to say thank you to this woman for helping her escape. Minty gave the woman the only thing she had to give, her quilt.

All that night, Minty walked north. At dawn, she hid in the woods. She listened for the sounds of dogs and slave catchers who might be chasing her. When she heard nothing, Minty fell asleep.

She continued traveling at night and sleeping during the day. After many days and nights, Minty finally reached the white farmhouse. She knocked on the door. A white woman opened the door, saw Minty, gave her a broom, and told her to sweep.

Minty was surprised. She was no longer a slave to be ordered to work! Suddenly, Minty understood why the lady had handed her a broom. If Minty looked like she worked for this woman, no one would guess she was an escaped slave.

That night, the woman's husband told Minty to get into his wagon. He covered her with blankets. He piled vegetables on top of her. Slowly, the farmer drove his wagon through Camden.

On the other side of town, he let Minty get out. He told her where to find the next station on the Underground Railroad.

Minty memorized his directions. Then she set off, once again using the drinking gourd as her guide. When she reached the second "station," Minty was given food and more directions. Again she memorized the way she was supposed to go.

Minty hid and slept during the day. She walked only at night. Finally, Minty saw a small stone marker along the road. The stone marked the border between Delaware and Pennsylvania. Pennsylvania was a free state with no slaves!

Minty stepped across the border into freedom. To honor this special moment, Minty changed her name back to Harriet, her mother's name. She was no longer Minty Tubman, a slave, but Harriet Tubman, a free woman.

Harriet said this later in her life: "When I found I had crossed that line, I looked at my hands to see if I was the same person. I felt like I was in Heaven."

8

Harriet Becomes
a Conductor

Now that Harriet was free, she had to find a way to earn money. She made her way to Philadelphia. She was amazed at the tall buildings. She stared at all the people shopping and working. She saw how African-Americans were treated equally.

Harriet worked in a hotel kitchen. She cooked. She washed the dishes. As usual, Harriet worked hard. She saved every penny she could.

Harriet met other people, both white and African-American, who believed slavery was wrong. She talked with William Still. William's parents had been slaves, but he had never been a slave himself. He was helping slaves escape. His group gave runaway slaves a place to stay. He gave them food and clothing.

Harriet met other runaway slaves like herself. One night, she talked with a man who needed help rescuing a mother and her two children. When Harriet heard their names, she jumped up in surprise. The mother was Mary Ann, her own sister!

Harriet said she would lead them to freedom.

Harriet learned how to safely travel to Baltimore, where her sister was hiding. When they saw each other, they were thrilled. They had never thought they would see each other again!

Harriet led them along the Underground Railroad. They rode in wagons. They walked. Finally they went in a boat across a river to freedom in Philadelphia.

This was Harriet's first trip as a conductor on the Underground Railroad. But it wouldn't be her last. Harriet Tubman had a plan. This

time, she would bring her husband, John, to Philadelphia.

Harriet spent the summer of 1850 working in a hotel. Once again, she saved every penny. She would use the money to help John come north.

That year, a new law had been passed called the Fugitive Slave Bill. The law said that any runaway slaves must be returned to their masters. Even northern states had to return escaped slaves. At anytime, someone could turn Harriet in to the police. Then she would be sent back to Maryland as a slave.

Harriet also knew it was very dangerous for her to return secretly to Maryland. If anyone found out who she was, she would be a slave again. But Harriet was determined to bring John Tubman north to live with her.

Harriet put on a man's clothes to disguise herself. She wore a big hat to hide the scar on her forehead. Very carefully, she made her way back south to Bucktown, Maryland.

That night, Harriet went to the cabin where she and John had lived. Harriet knocked on the door. John opened the door. He stared at Harriet. He was completely surprised she had returned. Harriet was surprised, too. John was not alone! After Harriet had run away, John had married another woman.

Harriet didn't say a word. Her heart was broken. She had loved John Tubman. But he had turned against her.

Harriet would never see John again. But she would return to the Bucktown area. Harriet became determined to rescue other members of her family. She would also lead other slaves to freedom if they had the courage to follow her.

On her next trip to Maryland, Harriet brought eleven slaves north on the Underground Railroad. One was her brother William Henry. Another was his girlfriend, Catherine. Catherine and William Henry wanted to be married. But Catherine's master wouldn't let her. So William Henry bought Catherine a man's suit for her disguise. Together, they joined Harriet's group and escaped to freedom.

But now Harriet had to take her passengers to Canada. The law against runaway slaves meant escaped slaves had to get to Canada before they could really be free.

This problem was a challenge for Harriet. But it was a challenge she was up to. She took her passengers on the long trip to Niagara, New York. There they crossed to Canada and freedom. Harriet rented a house in Saint Catherines, Canada. Harriet spent part of the winter in Canada before returning to the United States to continue her work.

9
Harriet and the Underground Railroad

In the spring, Harriet went back to working in hotels. She saved her money so she could go south in the fall. This was the best time to help slaves escape.

In 1852, Harriet began making at least one trip a year to the South. Some years, she made two trips. On each trip, she brought more slaves north to freedom.

Helping slaves escape was not easy. But Harriet used her wits to help. When she went south, she often dressed as a man. Sometimes she dressed as an old woman. More than once, Harriet's disguises saved her from getting caught.

One day, Harriet returned to Bucktown, where she had grown up. Harriet was afraid people in the area might recognize her. She dressed like an old woman and carried two chickens tied together with string. The chickens were part of her disguise. Harriet looked like a slave woman taking her chickens to sell at the market.

Harriet turned a corner. She saw a white man she recognized from the plantation. Harriet thought he might know who she was. Suddenly, she let the chickens go. The birds flew into the air. They squawked. They flapped their wings. Harriet chased after them as they flew over a fence.

The people in the street laughed at Harriet and her escaping chickens. But the white man walked right past Harriet. He had been so close, he could have touched her. Another narrow escape!

Still another time, Harriet was riding a train to Maryland. Two men came through the train car. They stopped and stared at

Harriet. Harriet guessed they might be looking for her. Even though she could not read,
Harriet pretended to be reading a book. She
prayed that she was holding the book right
side up! Luckily, she was.

One man said, "This can't be the woman.
The one we want can't read or write." The
men moved on.

When Harriet reached the area where she
was going to help slaves escape, she hid for a
few days. She let a few trusted slaves know
she was in the area. Then she waited until
Saturday night. This was the best night for
slaves to run away. The next day was Sunday,
when the slaves did not have to work. This
way the masters would not miss their slaves
until Monday morning.

Harriet told the escaping slaves to meet
her at a spot in the woods. The place was different each time. When the slaves found her,
she took command. They had to follow her
orders and do exactly what she said.

When the escaping slaves grew tired,
Harriet carried their children. When they

were scared, she sang songs to encourage them to keep going. If a slave wanted to turn back, Harriet would not let him or her. She said firmly, "Move or die!" Harriet knew that if one of her escaping slaves was captured, he or she might tell the secret of her route on the Underground Railroad.

Harriet had her own special routes north along the Underground Railroad. She knew which roads to take and which to keep away from. She found the best trails through the woods. She knew the easiest places to cross streams and rivers. She used the skills her father taught her to survive when she traveled alone or with a group.

Harriet knew which houses were safe stations on the Underground Railroad. She knew which stationmasters would provide food and shelter. When she came to one of these houses, Harriet knocked gently on the door. When someone asked who was there, Harriet said the secret passwords, "A friend with friends."

Harriet also knew the safest places to hide

if they were chased. She hid her passengers in old barns or sheds. She hid them in holes where potatoes were stored in the winter. Once she hid her passengers under a pile of manure. The escaped slaves breathed through hollow pieces of straw until the slave catchers left!

10
Harriet Tubman, the Moses of Her Race

Slave owners were very upset that someone was helping their slaves escape. Because Harriet often disguised herself as a man, they thought it was a man helping the slaves. Before long, they learned it was a woman named Harriet Tubman. They offered to pay thousands of dollars for her capture. But no one was able to catch Harriet Tubman.

The slaves gave Harriet a new nickname. They began calling her Moses. Moses was a man in the Bible who helped slaves escape from Egypt. Harriet called the South her Egypt. Harriet became the "Moses of her race."

Harriet had one of her most meaningful

adventures when she helped three of her own brothers escape. She went to Bucktown and found her brothers. It was Christmas Day. Their mother had fixed a special meal for her sons. But she did not know they were escaping with Harriet.

Harriet let her father know they were hiding in a barn. She did not tell her mother. Harriet knew her mother would be so excited to see her that she might accidentally let someone know her sons were running away.

Ben brought food to the barn. But he kept his eyes tightly closed. Ben always told the truth. After Harriet and her brothers escaped, Ben was asked if he had seen them. Ben answered honestly that he had not "seen" them!

Years later, Harriet helped her parents leave the South. They were too old to walk. So Harriet found a horse and wagon and drove her parents north. People gave Harriet money so her parents could take a train to Canada.

Harriet's work on the Underground Railroad

ended when the Civil War began in 1861. For ten years, Harriet had helped more than three hundred slaves escape along the Underground Railroad. She proudly said, "On my Underground Railroad, I never ran my train off the track and I never lost a passenger."

But Harriet's work was not done. She helped the Union Army during the Civil War. In 1862, Harriet went to South Carolina. She helped slaves who had fled to the safety of the Union Army. She found them food and clothes. She sold pies to earn money.

Harriet worked in a hospital, too. She nursed sick African-Americans. She took care of wounded white soldiers.

The Union Army found a special job for Harriet. Army officers knew about her skill in helping slaves escape the South. They sent her into the countryside to spy.

In the summer of 1863, Harriet was given a special mission. She went with some gunboats up a river in South Carolina. Her job was to find slaves and lead them to the boats.

More than eight hundred slaves escaped with Harriet's help!

The end of the Civil War in 1865 meant the end of slavery in America. But Harriet still didn't stop. She joined her parents, who were living in Auburn, New York. She took care of them. She planted apple trees and grew vegetables. Anyone who came to Harriet's door was given a place to sleep and food to eat. Harriet sold any extra vegetables she had.

Harriet agreed to tell the exciting story of her life. She told her stories to her friend Sarah Bradford. In 1869, Bradford's book, *Scenes in the Life of Harriet Tubman,* was published. Her friend shared the proceeds of the book with Harriet, who used some of the money to buy a home.

Another happy event took place in 1869. Harriet married a man named Nelson Davis. They shared a peaceful life together until he died nineteen years later.

Harriet still wanted to help African-Americans. She decided to make a home where older African-Americans could live for free. In 1896, she bought land. She gave the land to her church. In 1908, the church built the home Harriet had dreamed of. In 1911, Harriet herself moved into the home. She was about ninety-one years old.

Harriet had led a long and thrilling life. When she died on March 10, 1913, almost everyone in Auburn came to her funeral.

Today a large sign stands in Auburn in memory of Harriet Tubman. It highlights Harriet's accomplishments on the Underground Railroad and honors her work as a spy and a nurse.

Who would have guessed that little Minty Ross would one day be proudly called the Moses of her race?